The Magician of 1919

'Modern Chinese Masters' is a new imprint of short fiction from contemporary Chinese writers in English translation. Each title has been chosen for its ability to surprise and challenge preconceptions about Chinese fiction.

Cover illustration by Wang Yuankun.

The Magician of 1919

****

Christmas Eve

Two stories

by Li Er

Translated by

Jane Weizhen Pan and Martin Merz

With an afterword by Jane Weizhen Pan

Modern Chinese Masters

Make-Do Publishing,

Hong Kong.

All rights reserved.

© Preface, Li Er (李洱,) 2011.

© The Magician of 1919 (1919 年的魔术师,) Li Er (李洱.) 2004. English translation © Jane Weizhen Pan, 2011.

© Christmas Eve (平安夜,) Li Er (李洱.) 2003. English translation © Martin Merz, 2011.

© Looking at the World Through Li Er's Glasses, Jane Weizhen Pan, 2011.

English edition first published 2011.

No part of this publication may be reproduced, stored in a retrieval system or transmitted in any form or by any means electronic, mechanical, photocopying, recording or otherwise, without the prior written permission of the author.

ISBN 978-988-18419-6-4

Contents

Preface 9

The Magician of 1919 11

Christmas Eve 55

Looking at the World through Li Er's Glasses 95

Preface

The fourth of May 1919 is considered the dawn of modern China. It is now celebrated as May Fourth Youth Day. This day started with a fire, a fire that not only illuminated Chinese history but is also a significant event in world history. So who lit the fire? A magician. The magician of 1919. In my view, anyone who can change the course of history is a magician.

The Magician of 1919 was initially a chapter in my novel *Coloratura*. The magician and his nemesis Ge Ren turned out to have entirely different destinies — one is deemed successful, the other a failure. As a writer, I chose to sympathize with the latter. However, I still wonder what made the other person a success. Magic tricks?

Since the 1980s, Chinese people, especially young people, have developed a great interest in western festivals. Their fascination with Valentine's Day and Christmas far exceeds their interest in May Fourth Youth Day. *Christmas Eve* is about an old man's experiences on a Christmas Eve in China. Old men like Mr Chin are everywhere in present-day China. They were first dragged onto the treadmill of post-1980 reforms, then suffered the traumas of globalization. They find themselves hopelessly bogged down in a grim reality while enduring the collapse of their moral world.

I hope these two short stories, spanning two eras, will help you understand China's past and present.

I wish to express my gratitude to translators Jane Weizhen Pan and Martin Merz, and to my publisher Harvey Thomlinson for their efforts.

Li Er

2 July 2011

Elizabeth Huang

The Magician Of 1919

The Magician of 1919

On the fifteenth day of the Lunar New Year in 1919, a magician arrived at Bridge of Heaven, an area of Peking famous for astrologers, acrobatic performances, theatres and teahouses. The magician had few belongings except for a budgerigar and several pigeons he carried with him.

The budgerigar was a genius at languages. A master of both Chinese and English, the bird always rendered with fidelity, lucidity and beauty.[1] And because the bird's formative years were spent in Latin America, its Spanish and Portuguese were not bad either. Not only that, having had a long association with pigeons, the bird was fluent in Pigeonese — it could even convey the pigeons' egg-laying messages to its master. Within two weeks of arriving in the city, the bird picked up the Peking dialect. You would have thought you had bumped into an old Pekinese when the bird greeted you in an authentic Peking accent, high-pitched, filled with retroflex initials and final *er* sounds. This bird would certainly have become a stand-up comedian if it were alive today. Its previous owner, a shaman priest in a remote village, used to call it a 'Babel with wings'.

The magician called himself Bigshot Cowrie — people found out later that he was really Tian Han, who became a household name in revolutionary China.[2] Bigshot Cowrie hailed from Ching Geng town in Little Abandoned Hill. He took the budgerigar and pigeons with him when he left the town. It was not at all easy to find a spot to perform at Bridge of Heaven. But for a magician, it was not that difficult. At the time, the four chicks his pigeons had hatched were already mature enough to perform, so Bigshot Cowrie added a new show called Live Pigeons, Cooked Pigeons. At the end of the performance, he gave three of the

The Magician of 1919

pigeons as snacks to the two shop clerks at Wang's Offal Soup Kitchen. After that, the two clerks did not complain about the magician pitching his stall in front of Wang's establishment — anyway, the boss had gone back to Kalgan in nearby Hebei Province for a funeral and would not return for quite some time. Bigshot Cowrie's stall was just metres away from the East Intersection district of Bridge of Heaven, which was a prime location with plenty of passers-by. And so, in a cloud of offal soup steam, Bigshot Cowrie started his life in Peking. At night, he volunteered to clean pig intestines for the shop clerks so that he could stay overnight in the shop. At dusk, he emptied the shop clerks' chamber pot and doused his head with cold water — for the sake of his magic performance he shaved his head bald, so it was easy to rinse. After completing his morning ablutions, he took the budgerigar out onto the street to greet people with 'Morning, Grandpa', or 'Good morning! How do you do?' This served as a curtain-raiser.

A hat and a pair of large bell sleeves are essential tools of the trade for a magician. Bigshot

Cowrie was thus equipped too. What appeared to be just an ordinary hat in fact concealed a collection of tricks, and inside the side band was a rim fitted with a very long queue. The queue had been the compulsory hairstyle for all males during the Qing Dynasty, and the penalty for not having one was execution. After the fall of the Qing Dynasty in the early 1910s, men no longer had to wear a queue. Anyway, the queue, the budgerigar and the pigeons were Bigshot Cowrie's indispensable stage props. So there he stood on the street, and after a dramatic salutation to the crowd he landed the hat on his head like an experienced equestrian donning his riding gear. As the crowd slowly grew in response to the budgerigar's greetings, Bigshot Cowrie, with hands cupped reverentially and raised in front of his face, bowed to the spectators. 'Respected masters! Please cheer us on with a few coins if you've got some to spare. If you don't, I thank you for simply being here...'

He ended the introduction by daintily unfurling a rag he had purloined from Wang's Offal Soup Kitchen — magically, a pigeon appeared, cooing on the back of his hand. The crowd cheered. The bird hopped onto Bigshot Cowrie's hat and got to work. Suddenly, a queue grew from Bigshot Cowrie's shaven head.

'This queue,' he told me years later, 'was an invaluable treasure because it was like a cock — you could make it a stiffy or a softy at will.'

When it hardened, it would rise up slowly, just like the tail of a dog. Bigshot Cowrie assured me later that he was the only magician in the entire city of Peking who could do this.

Anyone who thinks that Bigshot Cowrie was set for a long stay in the Bridge of Heaven area is mistaken; magicians never linger because their tricks are limited and spectators' demands are not. Bigshot Cowrie learned this a long time ago, back in the days when he was still an apprentice in Guangdong Province in the south. So on the seventh day, he got up in the morning but did not empty the chamber pot. Instead, he shot off another round into it. Years later, Bigshot Cowrie likened this to a revolutionary act: a seemingly far-fetched interpretation, but not entirely wrong. Anyway, he grinned that morning when he heard the budgerigar's 'Good-night-and-see-you-tomorrow' directed at the two clerks who were still fast asleep. He knew he would never return; he had had enough of the smell of offal soup.

According to an article by journalist Kong Fantai, a direct descendant of Confucius, a group of local thugs ran after Bigshot Cowrie when he left Bridge of Heaven. Kong Fantai claimed that he had heard this from Ge Ren, a name that sounds just like the word for *individual* in Mandarin. Ge Ren, or *Individual,* participated in the New Culture Movement, in which Chinese scholars, including Lu Xun, advocated democracy and science as well as promoting social reforms. Both Bigshot Cowrie and Ge Ren came from Ching Geng town and had grown up in an orphanage run by foreign missionaries. Of course, Ge Ren himself had got the account of what happened that morning from Bigshot Cowrie. However, Bigshot Cowrie admitted to me years later that he had made up the story to win sympathy from Ge Ren in an effort to get help to settle in Peking. Bigshot Cowrie had heard about Ge Ren's return from Japan and that he was working in Peking, so he went to Peking to see Ge Ren.

This is what really happened that morning. It was early and most residents of Peking, even the hard-working stall owners, were still in bed, and certainly the lazy thugs were fast asleep. It was snowing. The street was quiet. The pigeons were still asleep, their heads resting under their wings, when Bigshot Cowrie carried them away. Only a few young wrestlers were in the street, practising the standing groin stretch. Their master, Zhao Kui, King of Wrestling IV, and his dog were standing nearby. The dog was not an ordinary breed. It had a legendary ancestor. Hu Biao, the previous King of Wrestling, had rescued the dog's grandfather from the clutches of soldiers of the Eight-Power Allied Expeditionary Force, which was stationed near the old Summer Palace. (Also known as the Gardens of Perfect Brightness, the palace was destroyed by British and French troops in 1860 during the Second Opium War and was further damaged in 1900.) The dog's grandfather was probably the only trophy the Chinese people had won in their wars with the west. According to a book titled *Curiosities in Bridge of Heaven,* the dog's daily diet included a few rabbits and two beef ribs. This treatise also recorded that because mating was not possible for the dog, it had developed a bad habit: it liked to play with its penis. To be precise, it liked to pass its tongue over its penis. After a while, the dog would become increasingly agitated, especially when it saw a stranger. But that morning, the dog seemed to be scared when it saw Bigshot Cowrie. It whimpered and attempted to run away. This was because of something hidden in the long queue that Bigshot Cowrie was carrying: several leopard whiskers. It was the concealed life force, the *Chi* of the leopard, infused in the whiskers that scared the dog. Now I am going to unveil a little secret: the whiskers were the source of strength that enabled Bigshot Cowrie's queue to stiffen up like the tail of a dog.

It must have been fate that created an invisible bond between a dog tail and Bigshot Cowrie. A few days after he left the Bridge of Heaven area, Bigshot Cowrie was following an antique dealer and stumbled into a *hutong*, one of many ancient alleys in old Peking. The *hutong* was called *gou yi ba hutong*, he was told, that is, Dog Tail Lane. On maps, the *hutong* has the more elegant homophonic designation of *gao ye bo*, or Loyal Gentlemen's Lane. Along the sides of the *hutong* were piles of old pots. By the way, the reason Bigshot Cowrie was following the man was because his refined looks reminded him of his childhood friend Ge Ren, the man whose name sounds like *individual*.

The man was scared at being followed by a bold stocky fellow with pigeons on one arm and a chained budgerigar on the other. Just as they walked past Grand Prosperity Fine Antiques, the man suddenly started to scream. Bigshot Cowrie later recalled that the scream was so forceful, a customer who was just stepping out of the store was thrown to the ground. The scream also startled Bigshot Cowrie and he bumped into a table outside the shop. Then came a crashing sound — the vases and bottles on the table fell to the ground and shards were scattered everywhere.

Many years later, Bigshot Cowrie found out that the bottles and vases he had thought not even good enough to use as pisspots were in fact priceless treasures. This was after he became the Communist Party secretary of the Little Bleak Mountain district. He learned this from a 'rightist', one of many educated people who in the 1950s were deemed critics of the government or to favour capitalism. This 'rightist' was a former antique collector. Only then had Bigshot Cowrie realized that the proprietor of Grand Prosperity Fine Antiques had not punished him excessively.

A Chronicle of Grand Prosperity Fine Antiques, issued by the Cultural Relics Publishing House, recorded the punishment applied to the penniless vagrant Bigshot Cowrie:

> *A servant used a chain to hang him on the old pagoda tree in the rear courtyard. The chain was not long enough for the stocky man and had to be extended with a section cut from the budgerigar's chain.*

Subsequently, the offender was lashed with mulberry twigs. The interrogation technique of Jia gun[3] was also applied in order to force the offender to kneel on sharp gravel.

This was the only physical punishment Bigshot Cowrie ever experienced during his life as a revolutionist. In fact, it is an exaggeration to call it physical punishment; it was more of a caution. The shop owner, Zhan Qinrong, was a Manchu. As an accomplished antique dealer, he could read people well. Finally, the shop owner realized that Bigshot Cowrie had not intentionally shattered his treasures and he ordered his servant to unchain the unfortunate fellow. Actually, Bigshot Cowrie should have thanked Zhan Qinrong for later allowing him to work in his store, fetching water and chopping firewood (unpaid, of course), for otherwise he would never have met up with Ge Ren again, and then he would have remained just another magician no different from an itinerant butcher, someone who offers his services to whomever needs a pig slaughtered.

Li Er

Whenever time allowed, Bigshot Cowrie performed his magic tricks in front of Grand Prosperity Fine Antiques, which attracted many customers to the antique shop. While watching Bigshot Cowrie's performance, antique dealers from 'five lakes and four seas' (to use Chairman Mao's later description) reached deals using the sign language of the trade — a series of concealed furtive finger movements inside the shop owner's sleeves. This is the origin of the policy of 'Fronting with cultural activities, backing with economic deeds', advocated by the Chinese Communist Government since the 1980s. In a very short time, Grand Prosperity Fine Antiques became the most bustling store in Dog Tail Lane. To use today's terms, this also secured the store's hegemonic position in China's antique-trading industry. Grand Prosperity Fine Antiques subsequently opened numerous branches all over China, and gradually formed its own WTO trading system. Of course, the Zhan family later was criminalized for its wealth; the rise of the family was because of a magician, and the fall of the family was because of the magic of history. It is said that 'magic leads to both success or failure', but this is not part of our story.

It was right in front of Grand Prosperity Fine Antiques that Bigshot Cowrie met Gu Hongming, an advocate of the monarchy and Confucian values, who was famous for preserving his queue even after the overthrow of the Qing Dynasty, when this male hairstyle was no longer compulsory. This was truly a historic moment — both for Bigshot Cowrie and for our nation. Unfortunately, the exact date of this encounter cannot be ascertained from the archives, and Bigshot Cowrie himself could not recall it either. Even *A Chronicle of Grand Prosperity Fine Antiques* contains only this vague description:

> *At the time, the willow tree in the courtyard sprouted young shoots. Rosy, the second daughter of the [Zhan] family, still had chilblains on her tiny hands. Icicles were still to be seen under the stuck-out tongues of the stone lions [at the front gate].*

The encounter was most likely in early March that year. According to the lunar calendar, it was sometime around the day of Waking of Insects, the sixth day of the second month of the year. Just as a well-trained pigeon landed on Bigshot Cowrie's hat, and the queue hidden in his hat came out and stiffened up like the tail of a dog, Professor Gu Hongming of the Peking University, a man with a genuine long queue, appeared. Bigshot Cowrie later recalled that initially he had not noticed Gu's queue, nor his red satin skullcap. Bigshot Cowrie's attention was directed at the blonde woman standing next to Gu Hongming. She was tall and slim, like a poplar tree, according to Bigshot Cowrie. Suddenly, the budgerigar uttered a few phrases of English, which must have been very idiomatic for both Professor Gu and the blonde woman instantly looked up to search for the speaker. The budgerigar then said something else. The blonde woman did not understand, but Gu Hongming did. He told her the budgerigar had spoken in Latin. The blonde woman was astonished. She gulped. Then she noticed Bigshot

Cowrie's dog-tail-like queue. By the way, this blonde woman was Emma Woodhouse,[4] a journalist for *The Times* of London. After squinting at Bigshot Cowrie's queue for a moment, she grinned and whispered something into Professor Gu's ear. What did she say?

Emma Woodhouse reported her whispered words in one of her articles:

> *I said to Mr Gu, 'Did you see that queue? Not even Leo Tolstoy would have created a coincidence like this.'*

Gu Hongming immediately frowned.

By then Bigshot Cowrie had noticed Gu's queue. Both men were annoyed as they thought that their trademark hairstyle was being copied by the other party. For Gu Hongming, his place in history rested on his queue. And for Bigshot Cowrie, the queue that he could transmogrify into a stiffy or a softy at will was his signature. It is understandable that he was annoyed at seeing another queue appear in the city of Peking.

Gu Hongming was a proud man. After his

initial surprise and anger, he stepped into Grand Prosperity Fine Antiques feigning composure. He did not have a lot of money on him that day but he felt he had to buy something. In the end, he settled on the shop owner Zhan Qinrong's tea set. The purple clay tea set was made in Yi Xing, a town in the eastern Chinese province of Jiangsu, famous for fine-quality teapots. Gu had to borrow money from his foreign friend. And since it was the foreigner who was paying, Zhan Qinrong felt compelled to overcharge, so he asked for a huge amount of money.

The tea set consisted of one teapot and four teacups, each engraved with the character 战, Zhan Qinrong's family name. In addition, the maiden names of Zhan's three wives were carved on three of the teacups, one for each wife.

With the newly acquired tea set in his hands, Gu Hongming suddenly found supporting evidence for polygamy, a custom he had always championed. 'See! It's a universal fact that a tea set comes with one teapot and several teacups. You would never see a tea set with one teacup and multiple teapots!' asserted Professor Gu on the steps in front of Grand Prosperity Fine Antiques.

In no time, the 'tea set theory' spread far and wide. Later, in an era when women's liberation was a hot topic, a feminist 'toothbrush theory' branched off from Gu's male chauvinistic theory. The woman who coined the 'toothbrush theory' was the talented Peking beauty Lu Xiaoman. Her romance with the great poet Xu Zhimo was one of the most famous love stories of twentieth-century China. 'Zhimo, you are not my teapot and I'm not your teacup,' Lu declared to her husband one day. 'You are my toothbrush, for a teapot can be shared but a toothbrush cannot — only I may use it.' This feminist 'toothbrush theory' would not have come into existence without the male chauvinistic 'teapot theory'. Thus we can conclude that the dog tail on Bigshot Cowrie's head indirectly kindled the development of feminist theories in China.

Anyhow, neither teapots nor toothbrushes were on Bigshot Cowrie's mind that day. All he was thinking was: *Who's that son of a bitch?*

Finally, Bigshot Cowrie learned from the son of a painting and calligraphy dealer that the man with the queue was a professor of the Peking University, not another magician. The painting and calligraphy dealer's son was studying law at the Peking University at the time. He later became assistant to the renowned legal expert Zhou Jihuai.

Let's go back to Bigshot Cowrie. After learning about Gu's background, Bigshot Cowrie's attitude towards the professor changed. He actually became fond of him. So fond of Gu did Bigshot Cowrie become that he even wanted to camp in the Peking University after learning the professor was the only male in the entire city of Peking who still had a genuine queue. Bigshot Cowrie knew spectators loved to watch his queue-growing show because they themselves, not so long ago, had queues too. He figured that if there was just one person in the university who sported a queue, then teachers and students would surely love to watch his show. However, Bigshot Cowrie had not expected to bump into Ge Ren. To borrow a famous quote from one of twelfth-century poet Xin Qiji's poems:

I've been searching and searching for someone all this time.

That moment I turned around, and there he was, sublime;

Ge Ren, there in a dimly lit street corner as if by design.

Of course, it is worth mentioning that there was another factor that brought Bigshot Cowrie to the Peking University: the budgerigar's feelings. The bird would only talk in English and Latin after its encounter with Miss Woodhouse and Gu Hongming. It reverted to its Chinese-speaking mode only after Bigshot Cowrie promised to go to the university to look for them.

At the time, the university was still located at its old site at Shatan in the inner city of Peking. That day, Magician Bigshot Cowrie, carrying his budgerigar, marched into the Peking University, the birthplace of the New Culture Movement in China in the twentieth century. According to

Bigshot Cowrie, someone who appeared to be a student warden was the only person who approached to ask the purpose of his visit. While Bigshot Cowrie racked his brain for an answer, the questioner became fascinated with the budgerigar. Finally, he turned his attention to Bigshot Cowrie. After scanning the magician from head to toe, he walked away with a smirk on his face. Bigshot Cowrie's ridiculous outfit deserved that smirk. It was cold but he was wearing what seemed to be summer clothes. His shirt had a pair of large bell sleeves. The sash was bright red. A pigeon was perched on his shoulder. There were white marks on his shirt — needless to say, they were pigeon droppings.

Bigshot Cowrie was lucky. It did not take him long to meet up with Ge Ren. At the time, Ge Ren was working at the university library. He had got this job through Li Dazhao, head librarian at the university and later a co-founder of the Chinese Communist Party.

The two childhood friends met on the steps of

the library. Ge Ren came out of the library and saw a magician performing. He stopped and watched for a while. Just as he was about to leave, a pigeon flew out of the magician's bell sleeve and landed on Ge Ren's shoulder. Suddenly Ge Ren heard someone calling his baby name in the Ching Geng accent: 'Ah Shuang! Ah Shuang!'[5]

It was not until his twilight years that Bigshot Cowrie acknowledged a fact: it was thanks to Ge Ren's introduction that he got his job at the university library. There is ample historical documentation that can prove this, even if Bigshot Cowrie had refused to acknowledge it. I will further discuss this point later. Now let me tell you what happened after Bigshot Cowrie saw Professor Gu Hongming for the second time, this time in the Peking University.

Ge Ren was very much interested in British poetry at the time, and was attending Professor Gu's class as an associate student. Bigshot Cowrie went with him the day after their reunion. Liang Song,[6] from Hangchow, also went along with them.

Li Er

He was a disciple of Kang Youwei, a scholar and prominent political thinker in the late Qing Dynasty. That day, Liang Song seemed to have something important to tell Ge Ren.

Bigshot Cowrie did not enter the classroom. He could never sit still, so he stood outside waiting for his friends, salivating because Liang Song had promised earlier in the day that he would take them out to the famous Quan Ju De restaurant for a feast of roast duck.

Bigshot Cowrie was attracted to the female students — to their ears, to be precise, their delicate ears, as most of them had short hair. Short hair was the hairstyle for progressive women in those days. The students gathered around Bigshot Cowrie because they were attracted to his birds. As Bigshot Cowrie's vanity began to swell, he performed his queue trick for them. As usual, he made a lewd face as the queue slowly stiffened. That look, which had always won him a chorus of cheers in Bridge of Heaven and Dog Tail Lane, did not impress the students — he looked ridiculous to them. The lasciviousness on his face intensified, especially when his budgerigar, the narrator, chanted the ditty:

As the tail of the magpie grows long

His mating need also grows strong

His mother may twitter

But still he will quit her

For a wife who's full-throated in song.

The girls must have thought he was a filthy pervert because the crowd dispersed immediately. Only a few girls stayed, pretending not to understand the ribald sketch. There were also a few old customers, people who had seen him perform before and were simply trying to figure out Bigshot Cowrie's secrets.

At the time, Gu Hongming was lecturing in a nearby classroom. For the few spectators who were familiar with Gu's comical look, Bigshot Cowrie's performance was particularly hilarious and they cheered as loudly as they could, as they would during a Peking Opera performance.

In response to the crowd's enthusiasm, Bigshot Cowrie performed even more energetically, and so did the pigeons. They flew back and forth between his bell sleeves and his hat. They worked so hard that they injured their beaks. How so? Let me explain the connection between the pigeons, the hat and the queue. As revealed earlier, there was a rim in the side band of Bigshot Cowrie's hat and the queue was fitted in the rim. Inside the red tassel on top of the hat was a small wheel coiled with very fine thread, one end of which was tied to the leopard whiskers hidden in the queue. The pigeons' job was to stroll around the tassel while holding the thread in their beaks to lift up the queue. Even though they appeared to be strolling leisurely, they were in fact working hard, as hard as if they were laying eggs. Because of the hard work, the female pigeon even gave birth prematurely — she laid a soft egg on Bigshot Cowrie's hat.

The class finished. Students streamed out of the classroom and saw Bigshot Cowrie's performance. His friend Ge Ren saw it too. There was no way he could stop the show because Bigshot Cowrie was totally immersed in his own performance. Ge Ren saw him remove his hat to reassure the spectators that he was bald. Then he put the hat back on ready to start another round of the show.

Of course, Gu Hongming saw this too. He quickly walked away. However, the fact that he did not stay does not mean he did not care about what he had seen. Otherwise, he would not have written the following words in a catechismal question-and-answer format in an article:

Where is heaven?

Heaven is in the nicest house on Jingan Temple Street in Shanghai.

Where is hell?

Hell is in a magician's hat in Peking.

The morning after that energetic performance, Bigshot Cowrie got up and noticed the budgerigar's vocalization was unusual. Ever since they had arrived in Peking, the budgerigar had been chattering away in either foreign languages or in the vernacular Peking dialect. But that morning, the budgerigar muttered some classical Chinese words in the manner of Professor Gu. These words sounded out of place in the Peking University, the cradle of the New Culture Movement, where vernacular Chinese was being promoted and classical Chinese was considered by some a dead language. Gradually, Bigshot Cowrie figured out what the bird was saying: 'Alack, alas, alack, alas.' Then he realized that two of his pigeons were dead on the floor, their bodies cold. Subsequently, he discovered that there was nothing inside his hat — the queue was missing.

Since Ge Ren had found him a job working in the university library, Bigshot Cowrie had slept in the library at night, and went back to Ge Ren's place only occasionally. The previous evening, Bigshot Cowrie and Liang Song had spent the night in the reading room. That morning, Liang Song was still asleep and did not wake up despite Bigshot Cowrie's repeated calls to him to do so. According to Bigshot Cowrie, he pinched Liang Song's nostrils together and forced the man to wake up through suffocation. He should not have done that as Liang was one generation his senior, but that morning Bigshot Cowrie did not care.

The two men quickly assessed this critical situation and came to the following conclusion: someone must have poisoned the pigeons and stolen the queue while everybody was asleep. As to why this person did not poison the budgerigar or take the bird away, there were two possibilities. Firstly, as the budgerigar went to sleep early and got up early, it always slept through the night and never got up to relieve itself or have a midnight snack. Secondly, the budgerigar wore a chain and there was a bell attached to the chain. The bell would have attracted attention if anyone had attempted to do something to the budgerigar.

So who would do something as cruel as this? Both Bigshot Cowrie and Liang Song thought about Gu Hongming. Bigshot Cowrie, remembering how Gu had left in a hurry the day before, was especially convinced that he was the culprit. At that moment, Bigshot Cowrie had an urge to grab hold of Gu's queue and mercilessly cut it off.

Another incident on the same day seemed to confirm Bigshot Cowrie's suspicion. At lunchtime, a librarian told Bigshot Cowrie that the university authorities had been informed that one of the librarians had a queue, which was undesirable, and that the person who had reported this was a certain Professor Gu Hongming. Cai Yuanpei, then chancellor of the Peking University, had ordered an investigation into the matter, with a report of the investigation to be submitted in a timely manner. According to the librarian, Gu Hongming had threatened to quit his position if the matter was not dealt with seriously. His colleague Chen Duxiu had been there too. Chen had pointed out to Gu that his demand was analogous to saying, 'It is alright for magistrates to burn down houses, while common people are not even allowed to light candles.' Chen, later one of the founding members of the Chinese Communist Party, was at the time an advocate of vernacular Chinese writing and a critic of traditional values, values that Gu was proud of.

This time, Gu Hongming did not fight back. Instead, he flung his long queue over his shoulder and praised his opponent by addressing him with his courtesy name: 'No one knows me better than Zhongfu!'

But Bigshot Cowrie's and Liang Song's theory was challenged by Ge Ren. Some other facts suggested that Ge Ren might be right. The first was that a cat was still alive after eating the dead pigeons. The cat was kept in the library to solve the rat problem. It was starving because it did not have an owner and only had Communist-style free meals. This style of communal dining was widely imposed on people in China during the Great Leap Forward period in the 1960s when communal dining halls were set up to serve free meals and people were not allowed to cook their own food. Millions died during the subsequent famine. Anyway, that day the cat entered the library reading room like a party cadre inspecting work progress and saw the two dead pigeons. The cat could not resist the lure of food, so it finished them off there and then. Not only was the cat not poisoned, the meal was so satisfactory that after feasting the cat fell fast asleep and snored away happily.

The second detail was that not so long ago Gu Hongming had organized a seminar on the queue issue. At the seminar, Gu had stated that the turbulent times the nation currently suffered from were caused by the demise of the monarchy. 'If you just mention the word "law", no one takes it seriously. But if you say "the emperor's law", people will be awestruck. It is the word "emperor" that matters.' Just as he was expounding this point, Gu fondled his queue and declared that he would keep his queue forever — the queue was the emperor's law. He then changed the subject. He said all the prostitutes in the Eight Laneways precinct loved his queue. Every time he went to this famous red-light district in Peking, the whores would fondle his queue like a chef prodding a fresh fish. Professor Gu ended the seminar with: 'Go your own way; let others talk.'

Judging from Gu's personality, he would not

have kept it a secret if he had in fact stolen the queue. The man was not embarrassed in the least to let people know about his excursions to bordellos — what did he have to hide? Ge Ren, however, believed a thief had stolen the queue. The queue was not the target. Instead, library books were. The thief had just taken the queue to tie up a bundle of stolen books.

But once the thought of cutting Gu's queue took root in Bigshot Cowrie's mind, it would not be uprooted, just as holes punched through paper cannot be unpunched. Bigshot Cowrie later told me that his hands became itchy whenever he thought about Gu Hongming walking around wearing a long queue on the back of his head.

One day in late April, Gu Hongming went to the library to borrow some books. At the time, Bigshot Cowrie was punching holes in past issues of magazines in order to bind them together. A pair of scissors was right there next to him. Bigshot Cowrie told me later that his fingers would not stop trembling that day, just as they trembled later, during wartime, when he had to pull the trigger of a machine gun. He said, had he decided to cut the queue that day, no one would have been able to stop him. But he did not do anything, as if he was persuaded by Ge Ren's analysis. He felt that he had to wait for a legitimate reason to act. Otherwise, he would have to let it go, even if he managed to grab hold of Gu's queue. He remembered Ge Ren had once told him that whoever cut Gu Hongming's queue would be on the front page of the newspapers, both in China and abroad, and would become more famous than Gu Hongming himself. Of course Bigshot Cowrie wanted to become famous. But he wanted to be famous for his performance, not for cutting off someone's queue. After all, what did this have to do with the disappearance of *his* queue?

And just like that, according to Bigshot Cowrie, he started tailing Gu Hongming. While tailing his target, he searched in his head for excuses to cut Gu's queue. If his own lost queue had feelings, it would have been deeply moved by its master's efforts. Bigshot Cowrie followed Gu Hongming to many places in Peking, from *shi cha hai*, a scenic lake area, to a favourite place of scholars, Tao Ran Pavilion, or the Pavilion of Joy, and to the old Palace in the Forbidden City. Once, Bigshot Cowrie even followed his target back to Dog Tail Lane. There he saw Zhan Qinrong, owner of Grand Prosperity Fine Antiques, pile teapots in front of Gu Hongming, but this time Gu did not buy one single piece.

One Sunday afternoon, Bigshot Cowrie followed Gu to the Eight Laneways area. At the time, Bigshot Cowrie did not know his journey to the land of brothels bore historical significance, as significant as his participation in the Communist Party's Long March in later years.

According to Bigshot Cowrie, his master during his apprenticeship down south in Guangdong Province had also liked to patronize whorehouses. But after the trip to Eight Laneways with Gu Hongming, Bigshot Cowrie realized that activities in brothels can be different depending who goes there. Gu Hongming's conduct in the brothels did not include the usual touching, and definitely did not involve unbuckling his belt. All he did was to ask the madam of the house to call the roll and he handed out money to each of the women as they strolled past, one by one. He laughed after handing out the last note, then simply left. Bigshot Cowrie thought this was fascinating (even more fascinating than his own magical tricks) as he followed Gu out of the Eight Laneways. He became even fonder of the man.

Finally, Gu Hongming noticed his tail. He waved to Bigshot Cowrie to come over. But Bigshot Cowrie turned around and walked away. A strange scene resulted: a man who looked like a monk being followed by a man who wore a long queue. To avoid attracting attention, neither of the men ran; instead, they walked briskly, 'as if the bottom of our shoes were greased', to use Bigshot Cowrie's words.

Gu Hongming quickly fell far behind, because Bigshot Cowrie at the time was still a virgin boy who had been performing magic shows regularly and thus had much more energy than Gu. Bigshot Cowrie occasionally slowed down a bit and looked around so Gu could catch up with him. Once Gu Hongming drew closer, Bigshot Cowrie accelerated to maintain a distance. A few times, he hid around corners to let Gu Hongming overtake him. Bigshot Cowrie did that not because he wanted to play hide-and-seek, but because he did not know his way back to the campus and had to depend on Gu Hongming. It was as if the two were repeating the hare and tortoise race. To Bigshot Cowrie, Gu's long queue was no longer his target. Rather, it was his signpost. If Bigshot Cowrie was the tortoise then Gu Hongming's queue was the hare's long ear.

The street became more and more crowded. In fact, it was exceptionally crowded — the street was teeming with people. Everyone was carrying a little flag. Bigshot Cowrie panicked whenever Gu Hongming's long queue disappeared in the sea of people and flags; Bigshot Cowrie really was like a tortoise that could not make its way back to where it belonged.

Bigshot Cowrie later admitted that, at the time, he did not know the momentous events he was witnessing were called the May Fourth Movement. In fact, he did not even know where he was. Only many days later did he find out that he was in the Legation Quarter of Peking. This tree-lined area was as pleasant back then as it is today. Amid the fragrance of the sweetly scented trees and the clamour of the crowd, Bigshot Cowrie got lost.

It was a beautiful day. Lu Xun, an influential figure during the May Fourth Movement, wrote in his diary: *May 1st, rain ... May 2nd, rain cleared ... May 3rd, windy at night. May 4th, cloudy.* The weather was perfect for taking to the streets: it was not raining, it was not windy, and the sun was not burning hot. But Bigshot Cowrie's mood was not as sublime as the weather. He saw many demonstrators holding flags with names of different universities, so he anxiously searched for flags from the Peking University. He was disappointed as there was not a single flag from his school. Of course, he did not know that students of the Peking University had been barred from leaving the campus.

The people's shouting became louder and louder. Slowly, Bigshot Cowrie realized that what they were shouting had something to do with the foreign powers in Shandong Province. So he joined the shouting. His slogan was the simplest: 'Shandong! Shandong!' But it sounded like the word in Chinese for *instigate*. The atmosphere was infectious, and his mood became infected by the thousands of 'Shandongs' reverberating in the air. He finally calmed down a little after breaking into Cao Rulin's residence and setting fire to Cao's bedroom.

Cao Rulin was a member of the Chinese delegation that had attended the Paris Peace Conference. The demonstrators were furious about the Treaty of Versailles, signed at the Paris Peace Conference, as a result of which former German concessions in Shandong were handed over to Japan instead of being returned to China. But Bigshot Cowrie did not know any of this when he lit the fire.

Li Er

In his twilight years, Bigshot Cowrie took delight in recounting his invasion of the Cao residence in Zhaojialou Lane. The building was similar to the one in which Bigshot Cowrie lived in his old age. Every detail was vivid in his recollections, even the shuttered doors and windows, the poplar trees in the courtyard, the insignia on the guards' uniform and the colour of the wall. The wall of the Cao residence was covered with Japanese creeper, which was like a green carpet airing in the sun. The wall of Bigshot Cowrie's house many years later was covered by layers of colourful slogans, like faded old posters. He liked to compare his home to Cao's when he revisited the past, as if it were only yesterday that he had stormed the Cao residence. Bigshot Cowrie used to point at the French doors in his living room and tell me he had entered Cao's house from there. I knew he was referring to how he had smashed a glass window and gained entry to the Cao residence.

Actually, Bigshot Cowrie was not the only one who smashed a window. According to historical records, students entered the Cao residence at the same time from more than one French door as they hunted everywhere for Cao Rulin. Bigshot Cowrie helped them, as if Cao Rulin had something to do with him. Then he saw the students transmitting in a relay a vat filled with some shiny liquid to one of the rooms, so he joined them. He could smell something fragrant in the air but he had no idea that the liquid was petrol. The last student in the line carried the vat from room to room; it appeared he did not know what to do with it. The student was skinny, and after a while he asked Bigshot Cowrie to help him carry the vat.

Suddenly, a woman's scream pierced the chaos. Then they saw a woman run out of a room. That was Cao Rulin's bedroom. The fire that later illuminated China's history and ignited Bigshot Cowrie's revolutionary life started in that bedroom. But at the time, Bigshot Cowrie did not care about the fire. His attention was focused only on a long queue that almost got burnt. The queue was hanging on Cao Rulin's bedroom door as if it was waiting for Bigshot Cowrie. Bigshot Cowrie could smell the dust on the queue when he tried it on. He escaped through the broken French door before the fire could catch up with him. To prevent others pulling at his queue, he coiled it around his neck.

At this very moment, the police grabbed him and were about to use the queue to tie him up. Bigshot Cowrie proposed they use his sash instead. At this critical juncture in the negotiations, Bigshot Cowrie's pants suddenly dropped to his ankles. It was the budgerigar, hidden in Bigshot Cowrie's bell sleeves, trying to be helpful by untying the sash on his pants. So a photo of a half-naked Bigshot Cowrie wearing a queue around his neck appeared on the front page of the next day's newspapers all over China.

The Times of London was the first newspaper in the west to report this news. The person who took the photo was Emma Woodhouse, the British woman Bigshot Cowrie had encountered in Dog Tail Lane. She wrote this caption for the photo:

Professor Gu Hongming harassed by the authorities on 4 May 1919, in front of Cao

The Magician of 1919

Rulin's residence.

But two days later, The Times published an amendment notice:

At the request of the Peking University, I would like to make further clarification: the person who was harassed by the authorities was in fact Professor Gu Hongming's best student. Both Professor Gu and the Peking University declined to divulge the name of this person.

— The Times correspondent Emma Woodhouse, reporting from Peking

Notes

---

[1] Yan Fu, the famous nineteenth-century Chinese translator who set these criteria for a good translation, would presumably have been happy with the bird's performance.

[2] Not to be confused with Tian Han (1898–1968), the activist playwright, translator and poet often called the founder of Chinese modern drama. In 1934, he wrote the lyrics for 'March of the Volunteers', which was adopted as the national anthem of the People's Republic of China. During the May Fourth Movement in 1919, Tian became famous for his part in the vigorous anti-

imperialist and anti-feudalist activities of the circle of artists and intellectuals he belonged to.

³ A technique that consisted of positioning three wooden or bamboo boards connected by rope around and between the suspect's bare feet. The construction of the device enabled the boards to be either snapped open and closed (like the wings of a butterfly) or gradually tightened. Each time the prisoner refused to testify or confess, the rope was pulled and the boards either whacked sharply at the ankles or slowly squeezed the feet ever more tightly.

⁴ Not to be confused with the character in Jane Austen's novel *Emma*.

⁵ The revolutionary poet and theorist Qu Qiubai, who translated the *Internationale* into Chinese, also had the baby name Ah Shuang.

⁶ It has not been confirmed as yet whether this person is in any way related to Liang Qichao, the collaborator of Kang Youwei in the reform movement of 1898.

Elizabeth Huang

Christmas

Eve

Christmas Eve

Whatever this festival was about, Mr Chin's routine never changed. Just after 6 pm on 24 December he made his way as usual to the railway station and the job expo building, which snuggled up against each other like Siamese twins. He wore a black and red striped scarf and a black woollen coat with magazines, newspapers and pirated DVDs tucked inside, making him seem potbellied and giving him a heavy, deliberate and authoritative look common to people of his age. His trustworthy bearing was inimitable. Around 10 pm he rode the subway back to the Bell and Drum Tower station. By the time he surfaced from the subway, hardly any of his merchandise was left and he looked energetic and much younger than his sixty-one years. At most, he looked like a man in his early fifties. If you saw him on the TV news, you'd think he was one of the younger generation of government officials that are called "the third echelon." And if you heard him sing 'Happy Birthday' in English in that deep voice of his, you'd be filled with admiration for an intellectual who had probably returned from overseas to serve his country. Come to mention it, he was an intellectual, though not one who had crossed the Pacific Ocean to return to his roots. Mr Chin was a retired schoolteacher from the suburbs who had come to the city to make further contributions to the nation. In any event, old people like him inspire respect. But in the light of the subway station entrance, Mr Chin appeared ill at ease. He looked lonely, sad, pitiful and a little edgy.

If I could just bring a girl back, what would it matter if I didn't sell any newspapers? At least I wouldn't feel like this.

Christmas Eve

Mr Chin's newsstand was west of the subway station on Tranquil Virtue Street, adjacent to the People's Square and a pedestrian overpass, directly across the street from the city's famous Garden of Eden nightclub. He ate, drank and relieved himself inside the newsstand, and had a collapsible bed under which he stored his cooking utensils.

That particular Christmas Eve, as he walked out of the subway station, he noticed it was snowing. Obliquely dancing snowflakes landed on his scarf and his chin became freezing cold. For no apparent reason, he recalled that whenever it had snowed during his childhood he'd thought of candy floss, the sort that resembles angora wool. It was a fleeting reverie, and he quickly turned his mind to the weather. *Foul weather like this will probably paralyze the railways, and maybe even cause a derailing.* The newspapers were already reporting such events, though only from overseas media so far, of course. For a moment he contemplated the consequences of a derailment, a catastrophe with Chinese characteristics: adults screaming, children wailing, and opportunistic looters profiting from the misfortune of others. He frowned and violently shook his head like a Pekinese dog, expelling the thought from his mind. Then Mr Chin contemplated the fate of the people who would be stranded in the train station. With the Lunar New Year fast approaching, they would have to pass the tedium of anxiety, frustration and sadness by reading his newspapers. He perked up when his imagination conjured up images of young girls stranded by a derailment, the sort of girls who were in no hurry to return home. As long as there was money to be made in the city, going home to see their families wasn't that important. After all, the Lunar New Year was still a few days off — plenty of time to make a bundle. If someone gave them a job that would help them strike it rich, they would gladly forgo a visit home for the Lunar New Year festival. And Mr Chin — their Uncle Chin — was precisely the generous kind of person who could make it all happen.

But where are these girls? thought Mr Chin. *Why wasn't I able to snare any?*

Christmas Eve

After ten in the evening, streetlights were usually few and far between. And in such dim light people could barely see where they were going. Yesterday's evening paper had reported that someone was walking along when, *poof!*, he disappeared. He fell down a manhole, and by the time he was fished out he was frozen solid like an ice block. That's what happened when there was dismal lighting. But tonight the streets were exceptionally well lit and many shops were working overtime. Even the shops that were closed had dazzlingly bright display windows. Upon closer inspection, Mr Chin discovered that even the mannequins were wishing everyone a Happy Christmas.

Christmas Eve? What's Christmas Eve? Mr Chin didn't really know.

On the way to his newsstand, he saw that all the lights in the square were switched on. If not for the swirling snowflakes misting up the night sky, it would have been as bright as day. Unlike most evenings, and despite the late hour, groups of people were huddled together on the square intermittently breaking into song. Another bunch of people on the pedestrian overpass were also singing, like quacking ducks being herded onto a bridge. When cars passed underneath, they hurled snowballs at them. But the drivers didn't get angry, and even honked their horns as if to join in with the singing.

When he arrived at the newsstand, he saw a neon sign over the door of the Garden of Eden nightclub flashing the words 'Merry Christmas'. Christmas again? He'd never heard of Christmas Eve before — was it a holiday sanctioned by the State Council? Apart from the chaos of wartime, there had never been a less safe time than the present. People really needed to pay attention to their personal safety and keep one eye open when they went to sleep at night. And it wouldn't hurt to keep another eye on your backside. Setting a new holiday was a big deal. Why hadn't the newspapers done anything to publicise it so that every man, woman and child knew about it and everyone could enjoy the holiday together?

Christmas Eve

As soon as he thought about people enjoying a holiday together, Mr Chin felt melancholy. He remembered his daughter. She had taken his retirement stash, run off to Fujian with her glib boyfriend and then snuck into Japan illegally. Just after she made it there, she'd died of a lung disease. The realization that she would never enjoy this strange new holiday saddened Mr Chin.

His daughter, forever a twenty-five-year-old girl, smiled at him from a photo in the corner of the newsstand — a computer-scanned enlargement affixed to the wall above the Panda brand cassette recorder. It had been taken when she was in her teens, when she was still just a girl. In it, she was pouting so hard you could have balanced a peanut oil bottle on her lips. She was frowning too, as if she didn't want to miss out on celebrating the Christmas Eve she would never experience many years later.

A dumpy lad in a leather jacket and ranger boots walked up to the newsstand. He had a crew cut and was clean shaven. A small golden cross sparkled on his chest. You certainly couldn't tell what he did for a living.

He asked if Mr Chin had a telephone he could use, flashing his mobile phone like an ID card to show the battery was flat and he was forced to resort to asking to use someone else's phone. Mr Chin got the message: since early this year it seemed that only paupers used public phones and the lad didn't want anyone thinking he was a pauper.

'There's a phone, but it's not a public phone,' Mr Chin told him. 'If it's really urgent, I can charge you public phone rates.'

The lad whipped his wallet out from his coat and produced a 100-yuan note, which he slapped down noisily in front of Mr Chin.

Well, this will be easy, thought Mr Chin. Nonchalantly, he held the note up to the light and examined the portraits of the four founding fathers of the People's Republic to verify it wasn't counterfeit.

Mr Chin overheard the lad wish someone a

Christmas Eve

Merry Christmas. 'Hurry up! Come out! Hiding at home on Christmas Eve. Don't be boring!' The lad arranged to meet the person in the Garden of Eden. Mr Chin couldn't hear what the other party was saying, but the lad's eyebrows jumped as he said, 'I just made a killing. I'll treat you to an oil massage. It's more fun with company.'

After agreeing not to leave without meeting up, the lad dialled another number and again wished someone a Merry Christmas. He then asked if the other party had received his SMS message.

Mr Chin wanted to ask what sort of a holiday Christmas Eve was. Luckily he didn't, because the lad would have sneered at him too.

The lad was reclining on the bench in front of the newsstand and laughing a nasally laugh into the receiver. Then Mr Chin heard him say 'S' and 'B' in English. He didn't understand what the lad meant at first, but then recalled that he frequently saw those two letters in newspaper supplements and it registered they were an abbreviation for *sha bi* and the lad was actually calling his friend a 'dumb cunt'.

'You SB, a frequent traveller like you and you don't know what Christmas Eve is? You must have heard of Jesus, or have you really turned into an SB? You know the movie *The Last Temptation of Christ* — you've seen the DVD, haven't you? The nude scenes are pretty good, though they could have done with an oil massage scene. Well, I'm treating you to an oil massage to make you more Jesus than Jesus. How about it? Give me a little face, OK?'

The lad dialled another number. It sounded like he'd called his wife, or perhaps his girlfriend. He was asking for some time off, almost begging for it. He had plenty of excuses. He said he was working on a big business deal. He spoke of a 'win-win situation', then brought in 'globalisation' and reminded her of the nation's foreign-policy objective of 'not interfering with the internal affairs of others'. Then he boasted that he was about to 'extort a huge sum', assuring her it was 'in the bag'. After going on like that for a while, he

Christmas Eve

changed the topic, telling her not to worry, that he would definitely never go to 'that sort of place'. If he did, his thing would rot and fall off, he said. The woman must have reminded him that it was Christmas Eve. Now he feigned ignorance. 'Christmas Eve? What's Christmas Eve? It's peaceful every night nowadays.' Then it was the woman's turn to call him an SB. Mr Chin saw the lad spring up from the bench, almost ripping the telephone cord out of the wall. 'What? You're calling me an SB! OK, fine. Look, my client's just arrived. Call me an SB, fine, I'm an SB. Bye-bye.'

But no customer had arrived. The lad immediately dialled another number. To Mr Chin's surprise, it was the Garden of Eden nightclub. He said he was just outside the door and would soon be bringing some guests. 'Do an advance screening for me. They've gotta be pretty upstairs and pristine downstairs. No compromise on standards, OK.'

Although Mr Chin didn't understand everything he overheard, he wasn't completely ignorant about Christmas. *Shit, it's that foreign holiday we call Peaceful Night because they're the first words in the Chinese song 'Silent Night'.* He remembered that the previous Christmas, which had also fallen at the end of the year, his daughter had sent him a greeting card wishing him a Merry Christmas. Nowadays, everything was changing. Things in China were changing, and changing into foreign things. Sometimes it was the same old wine in a new bottle, but often as not it was old wine in an older bottle. Like the square: just a few months ago, before May First, it had been the Pearl Square. On May Day, a gaggle of old ladies with red armbands gyrated through the Rice Seedling folk dances. Then the name had been changed to the People's Square. Did they lay down any new tiles? Did they plant any trees? No. And before International Women's Day, that nightclub across the road had been the Grand View Garden, a name taken from the classical novel *Story of the Stone* because that garden was famous for being home to beautiful girls. The nightclub had been busted during an anti-prostitution campaign, and when it reopened a week later, it became the Garden of Eden. The girls who worked there were still the same girls. Well, there was new batch of girls, but the biggest change had occurred on 7 November when a crew of Russian girls were brought in from Manchuria.

After the lad had finished his telephoning, he picked up a newspaper and began to read.

He must be waiting for me to give him some change, thought Mr Chin. But Mr Chin had forgotten to take note of the time.

'Hey, sir, how much change should I give you?' he asked.

'Old man, you tell me,' said the lad, looking up from the newspaper as he picked his nose.

The nose-picking made his voice sound raspy, which Mr Chin took to be unconcern. *He must be a generous person*, Mr Chin speculated, *otherwise he wouldn't be treating all those people to an oil massage. They use expensive imported French baby oil, and the value goes up astronomically by the time it's poured into the masseuse's palm and smeared all over the customer's body. And after the massage there's bound to be a little bit of something else too.*

One of the girls who had worked at his newsstand briefly before going over to the Garden of Eden to make big money had told Mr Chin: 'Oil massages are like greasing a machine, and men are the machines. After greasing, they're ready to launch, and they become airplanes. What happens after they're launched? They have to come down again. That's what we call shooting down planes.'

Mr Chin had been as ignorant about the meaning of 'shooting down planes' as he was about Christmas Eve. He couldn't make head nor tail of it for ages. Later, another girl had moved on from his newsstand to the Garden of Eden. After a few days working there, she'd become a battle-hardened veteran. Pointing to Mr Chin's crotch, she'd said without the slightest embarrassment, 'Shooting down planes means giving a hand job.' Mr Chin was so shocked he'd clamped his thighs together tightly.

Christmas Eve

Of course, nowadays he was no longer clamping his thighs. Not only that, from time to time when men came out of the Garden of Eden to buy newspapers from him, he even asked them the going rate for shooting down a plane. Mr Chin's jaw had dropped at the astronomical figure. *All they do is spread their legs and let the girl grapple with their thing till it gets soft again. The money I make selling newspapers for a whole month is only just enough to pay for one shot.*

Mr Chin was sure this lad was a patron saint of charity. *And seeing he's a charitable saint, I might as well extort a huge sum.* The words 'extort a huge sum' sounded familiar somehow, then Mr Chin recalled they were the very words the lad had used on the phone. *Yes, 'extort a huge sum'.*

To show that he himself was a person of status unconcerned with this trifling amount of money, Mr Chin noisily rummaged around with the coins when he opened the drawer to look for change, and deliberately let a few coins fall on the ground so he could make a show of not bothering to pick them up. As he did this, Mr Chin sang an English song quietly to himself.

After a few lines, he stopped singing and asked nonchalantly, 'Did you make any long-distance calls?'

He knew full well the lad hadn't, because he'd been watching like an eagle. He asked the question to let the lad know that he really had no idea exactly how much to charge and could only come up with a rough number. If the lad really were a charitable saint he'd just say, 'Forget it. Don't bother giving me any change.' If that happened, the wily Mr Chin would be sure to behave in an appropriate manner. He would say to the lad, 'I can't do that. The People's Liberation Army's Three Rules of Discipline and Eight Points for Attention clearly stipulate that we must be fair in commercial transactions. How about this? It's obvious you're an educated man who likes to read, so take something that interests you.'

Mr Chin's little daydream was quickly obliterated.

Christmas Eve

'Give me ninety in tens, I don't want any coins. And this looks interesting. I'll take it,' the lad said, folding the newspaper, 'Say, wasn't that pop star Liu Xiaoqing a real SB for staying in jail for over a year? This one here spilled all the beans after just a few days. Didn't Liu know about the policy of "leniency to those who confess and severity to those who resist"?'

Mr Chin didn't place the pile of change, which included fifteen yuan in coins, in the lad's hand. Rather, he nonchalantly plonked it on a bundle of newspapers, conducting himself like a chess master trying to anticipate his opponent's next move. The bundles of newspapers were stacked in disorderly fashion and a few coins fell between the cracks. Mr Chin did not look at his adversary as he made his move; instead, his gaze wandered off into the distance towards the People's Square, from where he could hear the occasional exaggerated shrieks of people frolicking. The hubbub brought to mind the girl who had left his employ two days earlier. Like the girl before her, she'd stayed at the newsstand for only two weeks, though she hadn't gone very far when she left. She too had gone to seek her fortune at the nightclub across the road.

As was the custom, the procuress — they used to be called Madam but now they were known as Mommy — had given Mr Chin a sum of money in accordance with the law. Mr Chin had signed a contract with the girl, whereas the procuress was poaching his employee: contract law clearly stipulated a fee had to be paid in such instances of recruitment. Indeed, the first thing Mr Chin did every time he hired a new girl was to prepare a three-month employment contract.

Mr Chin always made a point of taking his new employees for meals at the fast-food outlet below the nightclub, which was operated by the same people as the nightclub. At each of these meals, Mr Chin would criticize the girls who went upstairs to work in the nightclub after they'd eaten at the restaurant. But Mr Chin's reproofs carried a suggestion of something deeper than his ostensible tsk-tsking, a flicker of envy that bordered on admiration. Gradually, the component of admiration grew until it became apparent to anyone listening that Mr Chin was paying tribute to people who seized opportunity, who developed the economy and who moved ahead of others on the road to living the 'moderately prosperous life' newspaper headlines constantly trumpeted. His subtle words were most effective. Usually within a couple of days, the girls working at his newsstand would jump ship.

That was what the last girl had done just a few days earlier. Of course, she'd also paid him a sum for breaking the employment contract. Was it a lot? Not really, just 300 yuan. Mr Chin could count on a windfall like that every once in a while. And Mr Chin knew how to deal with the sort of girl who would consider welshing on him: as a precaution, he retained their ID cards. Without an ID card, a girl wouldn't get work even as a prostitute.

'After China joined the World Trade Organization,' the procuress at the Garden of Eden had explained, 'we have been obligated to integrate fully with international best practice. Customers have raised their standards, and the girls must likewise raise their professional standards. We must place emphasis on sincerity and keeping good faith, so no more passing off inferior goods and cheating customers. Now our clients don't just look for a pretty face or a petite waist, they can also examine the girl's ID card.' According to the procuress, the name and address on the front of the ID could be obscured with masking tape, but the date of birth must be disclosed to customers.

Watching the lad immersed in retrieving the coins, Mr Chin sighed. *He really is a bit stingy*, he thought. *If he were a little more generous, I would have gladly introduced that girl to him. I could vouch for her because she's only been working in the nightclub two days so she's guaranteed to be the freshest of all the girls in the Garden of Eden.* But now Mr Chin was hoping the lad would catch a nasty dose of the clap.

Mr Chin peered over the lad's head towards the Garden of Eden. The windows on the upper floor were tightly shut and the thick curtains prevented

Christmas Eve

any light from escaping. The walls of the building, and even the parking lot, were brightly lit, but the sky above the building was in total darkness. As Mr Chin took in this vista, his thoughts fell into disarray and his mind went completely blank. He planted his backside on the stool inside the newsstand. His vision became slightly blurred, and he stared uncomprehendingly. Gradually, he lifted his bottom off the stool, his mouth opening little by little in concert with the movement.

The lad told Mr Chin he was taking another newspaper because a coin had fallen through a gap in the piles of papers down into a join between the wooden boards below. Without thinking, Mr Chin picked something up and passed it out to the lad. The notoriously stingy Mr Chin didn't realise that what he proffered was not a newspaper but a pictorial called *Global Cinema Weekly*, which sold for 10.8 yuan a copy. At that moment, all his attention was directed at the silhouette of a girl who was approaching in a trishaw. She wore a red down jacket.

The girl disembarked, but didn't immediately dismiss the trishaw. She looked left and right, then lowered her head to stare at the ground for a moment, as if worried she had come to the wrong place. After a while, she finally paid the trishaw driver. She didn't walk towards the Garden of Eden, nor did she proceed to the pedestrian overpass, even though she appeared to be walking. That is to say, this young woman was virtually marking time in the middle of the road where she had dismounted from the trishaw. Mr Chin concluded in an instant that the girl was inexperienced and it was the right time to take action. Just as he considered that he ought to call her over, he found himself actually walking out of the newsstand and at the same time heard himself singing that English song again.

'Forgive me, miss, but you can't really blame me — after all, you bumped into the gun muzzle,' he whispered to himself as he walked towards the girl.

When he reached her, Mr Chin stood between

Christmas Eve

her and the Garden of Eden so that no one in the nightclub would be able to see her. *That procuress has eagle eyes*, thought Mr Chin, *and if she sees this girl there'll be no end of wrangling over who found her first.*

Mr Chin swallowed hard to prime his vocal cords to produce the tone he had employed innumerable times before. 'I noticed you standing there,' he said. 'Are you waiting for someone? It's freezing out here. Why don't you wait inside?' And he pointed towards his newsstand. The sign atop the newsstand, clearly illuminated by the lights across the road, read 'Little Bell'.

'See that,' he said. 'My daughter's name is Tink so she called her newsstand Little Bell.'

As Mr Chin spoke these words, he hadn't yet seen the girl's face. She seemed interested in what he said and turned her head to look at the newsstand. When she turned back to smile at him, Mr Chin saw her face. It was the face of a child, perhaps eighteen or nineteen, fresh and delicate. Mr Chin was struck by how beautiful she was; not extraordinarily beautiful, yet of a kind that was almost otherworldly.

The girl sniffled and, apparently embarrassed for having done so, lowered her head. Mr Chin found the sound of her sniffles very pleasant, like the sound his daughter made sucking her little feet when she was an infant. It was all like a dream, but when had he ever had a dream like this? Never. Especially after the death of his daughter; now he dreamed only of her grave mound and the sound of her weeping inside her tomb. *Damn, I've never had a good dream, not once.* He usually awoke in a fright, completely soaked in sweat, drenched like a chicken dunked into a bucket of hot water and about to be plucked. Once, he did actually have a good dream. He saw himself, having finally made enough money, on a boat to Japan, where he opened his daughter's tomb and saw her ashes. He collected her ashes and sailed back to China. Watching the bow of the ship plough through the waves, he knew that his daughter had finally come back home to his side. He should have been happy, but he'd suddenly burst into tears and woken up bawling.

When the girl raised her head again, Mr Chin saw that some snowflakes had settled on her long eyelashes, fluffy and glittering, with a breathtaking, mysterious beauty. Mr Chin began to stammer as he mentioned his daughter again. 'T-T-Tink. My daughter's name is Tink. I'm looking after the newsstand for her.'

What's wrong with me? wondered Mr Chin. Never in his life had he been so nervous. He'd seen pretty girls before. Why, the girl who delivered newspapers every day was very pretty. She'd recently graduated from the Postal Academy and had just learned to ride a bicycle. Once, she'd been unable to brake in time and had fallen into Mr Chin's arms. When he helped her up, one of his hands had somehow inadvertently slid under her shirt and snagged on her bra strap, which had snapped as a result. He hadn't been nervous then, and had actually found it funny. *Come on*, he'd thought at the time, *a bra strap isn't worth grabbing. You want to grope what's inside the bra, even if it results in a tongue-lashing.* Afterwards, he could be playfully boisterous with her, and if he gave her an ice-cream cone he was able to caress her cheek without any trouble.

When he was courting Tink's mother, he'd been the epitome of confidence. He'd get going on his interminable, grandiloquent rants about Ke Xiang, the star of a revolutionary model opera, or Guo Fenglian, the female brigade leader of the model agricultural commune Dazhai, then pontificate about Chairman Mao's first big character poster, titled *Bombard the Headquarters,* which marked the beginning of the Cultural Revolution, and then move on to denouncing the Soviet revisionist leader Nikita Khrushchev. Tiny beads of spittle would fly through the air and white froth would form at the corners of his mouth, rendering his father-in-law completely dumbstruck. But now, this girl, a total stranger, had him stuttering and stammering. It had all happened so suddenly and she had caught him off guard.

Mr Chin stepped back, and as he retreated

Christmas Eve

towards the newsstand he struggled to say, 'I-I-I'm going back there. It's really c-c-cold. I'm f-f-freezing.' He patted his face as if his weathered old dial was susceptible to ice-overs.

The girl fluttered her long eyelashes, apparently oblivious to his intent. She wasn't alone in that because Mr Chin himself wasn't sure what he was up to. As he retreated, the smooth carpet of snow seemed to become potholed and pitted, causing him to stagger and almost fall. He found his footing, but just as the girl came over to hold his arm, the harder he tried to stay upright the weaker his legs became. Suddenly, Mr Chin was facing the sky, floating as if ascending towards the clouds. But then he plummeted rapidly to execute a hard landing. After making landfall, he felt himself bounce up. He bounced up as lightly as a bird's feather, but fell again as heavily as a dead dog.

Mr Chin had no idea how he returned to the newsstand. He could only remember the girl holding his hand and pulling him towards it. Her hand was so soft, he couldn't sense any bones; it was just like candy floss, candy floss as soft as angora wool. He recalled that when his daughter was small she'd loved to eat popcorn and candy floss, a little of which she would apply to her fringe before running off to play with her friends.

Mr Chin became aware of a sweet taste in his mouth. He swirled his tongue around his mouth, but as he did so he sensed another taste: blood. After a shivering moment, he felt the world spinning and the wire-framed cot bed beneath him heaving like a flying carpet. The girl sat on the stool looking down at him. He could feel her breath. It was sweet. *No mistaking that*, thought Mr Chin, *it's the scent of candy floss.*

'You're drunk,' said the girl. 'Old men are like children when they get drunk.'

'More like a shameless dog, if you ask me,' said someone. The voice came from outside the newsstand. Mr Chin recognised it: the lad who had used the telephone. *Why hasn't he buzzed off yet?* wondered Mr Chin.

The lad spoke to the girl. 'This old deadbeat is

a real pest. Stay away from him. Don't let him ruin your Christmas Eve.'

Mr Chin wanted to tell the girl that he hadn't drunk any alcohol that night. He had the previous night. While he was trying to collect from the procuress at the Garden of Eden the 300 yuan stipulated in the contract, she had treated him to a drink and even arranged for two girls to drink with him. One was the girl who had just left his employment. Together they'd drunk a whole bottle, and though the wine had tasted like cheap rice wine well past its expiry date and adulterated with some aged fermented cooking vinegar, the procuress had insisted it was a genuine French red. A bottle like that cost 2000 yuan at the Garden of Eden, so on a per-person basis, even after a 20 per cent discount, it would cost at least 500 yuan, and when you took into account the hostess charges, you wouldn't get away without paying at least 1000 yuan. *Damn*, Mr Chin had thought at the time, *she's acting as if she's being merciful for not asking me to pay extra.*

Mr Chin sat up, his hands supporting his lower back. He decided to pour a glass of water for the girl from the thermos flask he kept under the cot bed. As he sat up, he saw that the lad was still outside the newsstand. Mr Chin suddenly came to a shocking conclusion: this girl could be the one the procuress at the Garden of Eden had mentioned, summoned from her home during the candidate-screening process that the procuress had worked so hard to develop. If that were the case, then that lad outside would be the girl's client. Mr Chin's mind fell into chaos for a moment, and his hand didn't seem to obey his instructions, the water sloshing out of the mug and soaking some newspapers on the floor.

Mr Chin soon discovered that he had misunderstood the girl. He could see that despite the lad's flapping tongue and meaningful glances, the girl was completely ignoring him. Soon Mr Chin heard a commotion outside as the lad's friends met up with him. After they had departed, Mr Chin heard the girl let out a long sigh of relief. Then he heard her speak to him.

Christmas Eve

'I'm here because I'm looking for someone. You were right, Uncle, I am looking for someone.'

'I could tell as soon as you appeared,' said Mr Chin.

'Really?'

'If I'm lying,' said Mr Chin, 'I'm a puppy dog.'

He could have said 'dog', yet he said 'puppy dog' because being with the girl made him younger, as if he had spontaneously dropped a whole generation in age. He noticed that every few minutes the girl cast a glance outside. *Surely*, Mr Chin thought, *she must be looking out for her boyfriend. She's such a nice girl; why would her boyfriend hang out in such a wicked place? When he eventually comes out, I'll give him a good talking-to.*

Despite what he was thinking, Mr Chin said to the girl, 'Isn't it Christmas Eve? Perhaps he's gone in there to sing with some friends. People don't necessarily fool about when they go to places like that. You can drink tea in there, or sing, or get a massage, take in a movie or just watch TV. I watched the Sixteenth Communist Party Congress in there. I'm sure a nice girl like you has a fine, upstanding boyfriend. He wouldn't betray you and engage in unspeakable acts in there.'

The girl covered her mouth with her hand to laugh. She didn't say anything about her friend. Out of the blue she asked Mr Chin, 'What about your daughter? She must be a good girl. Is that her photo? Look at that grimace. She must be a naughty little thing.'

Now it was Mr Chin's turn for a bitter laugh. 'Wait a moment,' he said while he got the photo down from the wall. He looked at it for a moment, then put it to one side and switched on the Panda brand cassette player. After a distorted cacophony, a young woman's voice began singing 'Happy Birthday'. The girl listened for a while, then giggled. But when she saw Mr Chin listening so intently, she turned her head to the side and pretended to listen closely with him.

After an age, it was over and the girl said, 'She's got a good voice, but she got the words wrong in a few places. Sounds like she's only a teenager, so she'd better call me older sister out of respect. Some day I'll teach her how to sing it properly.'

'You can sing that song?'

'I'm an English teacher in a private kindergarten,' said the girl. 'All my students can sing that song.'

If that's true, thought Mr Chin, *then Tink probably did get it wrong.* But ever since his daughter had left with that boyfriend of hers, this tape recording was Mr Chin's only solace. She'd sung it for him on his birthday last winter. The same day, she'd sent a car to take Mr Chin to the Drum Tower Hotel, where she'd booked a private room in the restaurant. It was only after he'd entered the room that he'd realised the middle-aged man who'd driven him there, that slippery-tongued rogue, was in fact her boyfriend. The man, with his swept-back coiffure ineptly imitating the style adopted by several national leaders, had chomped on a huge cigar, his elbows raised flush with his mouth. He and Mr Chin's daughter both wore rings with identical emeralds, like a pair of parrot's eyes. Mr Chin had drunk too much that day. He remembered when the birthday candles were lit, his daughter and that man sang that song for him. A few days later she'd handed the newsstand over to Mr Chin and run off to Fujian with that man, leaving only the cassette tape behind.

Of course, Mr Chin could not tell the girl sitting on the stool beside him any of this. Nor could he tell her that his daughter was dead and that he was constantly racking his brain for ways to make enough money to retrieve her remains.

'If only she could have met you earlier,' responded Mr Chin ambiguously. He had not expected the girl to be so shy, though soon her shyness turned into mischievousness.

'She probably did it deliberately,' she said. 'You wouldn't know the difference, anyway. When you were singing earlier, I could tell you were just making it up as you went.'

She had a pert air about her, and looked just

like a proud little princess. Mr Chin was head over heels for this girl, to the point of obsession.

The girl continued to cast occasional glances towards the Garden of Eden. She seemed to be waiting for someone — someone, like a mouse afraid of a cat, who would never come out. *It would be best*, thought Mr Chin, *if that scoundrel stayed in there forever so I can keep enjoying the company of this lovely girl.* To him she was even more adorable than his own daughter. At the same time, he wanted that scoundrel to appear as soon as possible because he couldn't bear to see her get hurt.

'Is your boyfriend a soccer fan?' asked Mr Chin. 'They're probably screening a soccer match. They usually go on till quite late.'

'Boyfriend?' said the girl and giggled. 'My boyfriend is overseas. I'm going to America next year to study there with him. I don't want to use his money, I want to pay my own way.'

'Then who are you looking for?'

'I'm looking for a very kind old man.' She

hesitated a moment, then summoned up her courage and continued. 'A friend told me to come. She is a former colleague. If I'm not mistaken, she used to make phone calls to me from here. She's gone overseas, but not to America, to England. She's celebrating Christmas Eve in Liverpool right now. She called and told me there's an old man who runs the Little Bell newsstand. She said, "You just need to work at the newsstand a few days and the old man can help you get the best job there is." She told me, "He's the most warm-hearted person in the world." Uncle, she was talking about you, wasn't she?'

'Me?' Mr Chin's eyebrows shot up.

'Yes,' said the girl. 'Aren't you that kind old man?' She seemed unaccustomed to this kind of flattery and shyly hid her face behind a sheet of paper as she spoke.

'Me?' shouted Mr Chin abruptly. 'No, not me!' His voice was very loud and he winced with the strain of the effort. 'That's not me. I'm not Mr Chin. Mr Chin is not me.' He was almost beating

Christmas Eve

his breast and stamping his feet.

He grabbed the girl's hand and tried to drag her out of the newsstand. The girl, a bewildered look in her eyes, pleaded with him to let her stay. By now, Mr Chin had managed to exit the newsstand. His lips were still moving but his voice had become extremely faint. 'I'm not me,' he mumbled over and over again. He was blocking the small doorway as if wanting to prevent the girl from going out into the street. The bright lights outside the newsstand illuminated his silhouette as he slowly fell to the ground. Looking up at the sky as he fell, Mr Chin thought it resembled a huge, black wok lid, though the streets all around were dazzlingly lit up.

He couldn't know then, nor, of course, would he ever know, that from that day on, and not just in the city of Hanzhong, but in every city in China, those festive lights would burn from the western holiday of Christmas to the New Year's Eve that is celebrated around the world, and remain brightly lit right up until the Chinese Lunar New Year in

February and through to the Chinese Lantern Festival fifteen days later.

Elizabeth Huang

Looking at the World Through Li Er's Glasses

Jane Weizhen Pan

Looking at the World Through Li Er's Glasses

'*The piercing feeling I have about intellectuals is their powerlessness — it haunts them every second. They are so powerless that they don't even have the strength to sigh.*'

— Li Er[1]

Li Er lives in a modest but pleasant compound in Beijing, not far from China's traditional intellectual hub, Peking University, where Bigshot Cowrie in *The Magician of 1919* met his friend Ge Ren and - like the young Mao Zedong - worked as a librarian.

While translating *The Magician of 1919*, I called Li Er with a list of questions about his characters and his views on writing. Harmless enough, I thought.

However, after artfully evading my questions for a while, Li said, 'Look, we'd better not talk about it over the phone, otherwise we'll be cut off. Let's talk face to face when you next come to Beijing.'

I persuaded him to stay on the line and we continued our conversation, but as he was talking about the role of magicians in his novels, the line went dead. Perhaps it was just a technical problem...

I called Li Er back. 'I told you so,' he said matter-of-factly.

A prolific talent, Li Er has published two novels, five story collections, seventeen novellas and dozens of short stories. His experiments with narrative form have earned him a reputation in Chinese literary circles as an avant-garde writer.

In 2003, in a strong field, Li Er's first novel,

Coloratura (花腔) (2001) won him the inaugural 21st Century Ding Jun Biennial Literary Prize. The judges commented: 'The author's masterful ability in utilizing the rich language resources obtained from historical and cultural sources is astonishing. The book is a 20th century history of China in a literary sense.'[2]

The Magician of 1919 was initially conceived as part of *Coloratura* but was published as a stand-alone piece before the completion of the novel. Like its 'parent work', *The Magician of 1919* exemplifies Li Er's fascination with the connection between Chinese intellectuals and the revolution, and how that connection is recounted in history, in which process the voices of individuals are often lost or distorted.

The Magician of 1919 is set during the turbulent times of the Warlord era in China. Student demonstrations in Peking on 4 May 1919 against the high-handed treatment of China in the Treaty of Versailles were a momentous event in modern Chinese history, and the government's suppression of the demonstration resulted in a more radical approach among many Chinese intellectuals, including Li Dazhao and Chen Duxiu, later co-founders of the Chinese Communist Party, who were working in the Peking University at that time. Li Dazhao was the head of the Peking University library in 1918 and 1919 when Mao Zedong was working there as an assistant librarian, the position also held by Bigshot Cowrie in the story.

By conflating real and fictitious historical events, both *The Magician of 1919* and *Coloratura* demonstrate Li's enthusiasm for narrative experiment. Some of the most apparently bizarre details of *The Magician of 1919* are not, in fact, made up: Gu Hongming's queue, for example. At the time, a real Professor Gu was teaching at the Peking University and his queue caused quite a stir on campus because in those days having a queue was considered a symbol of refusing to make progress. Gu, however, famously said to those who laughed at him: 'Yes, there is a visible queue on my head, but there is also an invisible queue in your brain.'

Both *The Magician of 1919 and Coloratura* are about recounting 'historical truth' — a truth that very much depends on who is speaking. And sometimes, the speakers have a foreign accent. For instance, both works contain foreign characters, including journalist Emma Woodhouse in *Magician*; and Ellis, a missionary, and Dr Kawada, an expert in faeces, in *Coloratura*. Li Er explained that foreign influences have been a vital part of Chinese history since 1840. 'Foreigners, especially westerners, hugely influenced the creation of China's modern image,' Li told me. As for how he chose the names for his foreign characters: 'I just made them up.'

'If you liken truth to the heart of an onion and look for it,' said Li Er in an interview, 'you will find there is nothing. However, that doesn't affect the taste of the onion — as you peel the onion to look for the truth, every layer of the onion will irritate your eyes in the same way.'[3]

In *Coloratura,* Li's innovative approach

intertwines faux historical documents, fabricated archival materials and fictitious interviews with descriptions of genuine historical events. *Coloratura* revolves around a secondary character from *The Magician of 1919*, the revolutionary intellectual Ge Ren, whose name is a homophone of the Chinese word for 'individual'. Breaking with a linear narrative, Li explores Ge Ren's life through the eyes of three narrators, each of whom has a different background, lives in a different era and has a different connection with Ge Ren. Li's experiments with narrative are already recognized as one of the more significant achievements of recent Chinese fiction.

Li Er, born in 1966 in Jiyuan, in Central China's Henan Province, attributes his decision to pursue a literary career to the influence of his grandfather and his father. 'My grandfather was very familiar with the Chinese classics and could recite sections on demand,' Li told me. 'The atmosphere in my family encouraged me to develop a love for books.' Li's father used to teach Chinese in a high school and secretly wrote stories as a hobby.

A family connection also informs Li Er's interest in writing about the role of intellectuals in history and politics. As a young idealistic student, Li's grandfather went to Yan'an to join the revolution with two of his brothers. At the time, many Chinese intellectuals were disappointed with Chiang Kai-shek's Nationalist government; they journeyed to Yan'an to support the Chinese Communist Party, in the hope of building a better China. Li's grandfather worked in the Marx-Lenin School, established in 1938 to train Communist Party cadres, but a trip back to his hometown to attend a funeral changed his fate. After the funeral, his family did not permit him to return to Yan'an. This decision became a political stain on Li's grandfather and took a huge toll on his life and the family. He became a natural target in his village during every political campaign after 1949, and suffered miserably. There was no communication between Li's grandfather and his brothers for three decades after this.

The desire to 'be closer to literature' brought Li Er to the East China Normal University in Shanghai, which, in the 1980s, had 'the best department of Chinese literature in China,' he recalls.

The 1980s was an important era for China, and for Li Er. In December 1978, Deng Xiaoping announced a new 'open door' policy to encourage foreign investment in China, and this embracing of western culture by the top leadership resonated throughout Chinese society. Creativity flourished.

Li Er described the 1980s as his 'cultural childhood; and for contemporary Chinese literature, the 1980s was its youth. That time in our history was like the first days of married life for newlyweds.'[4]

'Apart from what was available in my textbooks and some Russian novels, I did not have a chance to read foreign literature when I was in primary school or at high school,' Li Er told me.

'China at the time was just opening up, and university campuses were bursting with new ideas. I became a fervent reader of translated western literature as soon as I entered university. As for literature, the works of the 1980s were full of vigour. Like youths, writers at the time were rebelling against conventional styles and voices — we constantly wanted to try something new.'

Li's own structural innovations are solidly founded on a masterful control of language, and his approach involves an exacting economy with words.

'There are things that cannot be described with words. You can only *expose* those things through what you write. It's like the technique of leaving blank space in traditional Chinese painting,' Li told me. 'I write seven to eight hours a day but I'll be over the moon if one thousand characters can survive in the end. I'm slow. Things such as where-should-I-place-this-sentence take up a lot of my time.'[5]

Li Er's kaleidoscopic narratives can be seen as

an aesthetic response to the perplexing reality of modern China. Over the past thirty years China has undergone dramatic changes that can sometimes be experienced as painful, puzzling and even absurd. In Li Er's addressing of this perplexity, he demonstrates his surgical approach and mindfulness of the dangers of reaching conclusions lightly.

In Li's short story *Christmas Eve,* Mr Chin, a retired schoolteacher, makes money by working as a pimp and yet doesn't even know that 'shooting down planes' is a service prostitutes provide to men. While trying to make sense of life's confusion and absurdity, Mr Chin, like many intellectuals in China, becomes part of the absurdity himself.

Li Er's surgical approach is also evident in his 'rural novel' *A Pomegranate Tree Sprouts Cherries* (石榴树上结樱桃) (2004). The story of *Pomegranate* centres on a village mayor attempting to enforce China's 'one child policy' in the village while she is also campaigning for re-election. Li's ability to ridicule and his playful language make *Pomegranate* a deceptively light-hearted read. However, beneath its light-hearted surface, the novel explores Li Er's characteristic themes of pain and absurdity. Li says of his preoccupation with these themes: 'The life we live today requires one to anaesthetize oneself if one wants to feel happy. However, literature requires a writer to be sensitive. When I write, I'm true to my feelings. I live in a time when most of my feelings are pained. So if I choose to be happy, it often means I'm giving up, I'm bowing to the status quo. Therefore, when I write, I must not only express myself but also examine what I write. It's like a surgery, and I'm the surgeon and the patient at the same time.'[6]

Another of Li's great subjects is the Chinese intellectual. He writes, sometimes mockingly, about the environment in which Chinese intellectuals live, critically delineating instances of their cowardice, their pathetic self-importance and their powerlessness. During decades of Maoist political turmoil, the imperatives of survival often dictated that Chinese intellectuals consciously disabuse themselves of intellectual scruples. Since the 1980s, 'to be rich is glorious' has become China's national preoccupation, and scandals involving plagiarism, degree falsification and professors involved in dubious business enterprises have been cited as evidence of a morally bankrupt society.

The main character of *Christmas Eve*, Mr Chin, a retired schoolteacher, is an example of an "intellectual" torn between the demands of survival and morality. Mr Chin's retirement income is surely not enough to provide him a decent life when prices are soaring. To survive, he works as a pimp — a sideline that certainly generates more money than selling newspapers. And yet he is struck with guilt as he attempts to lure an innocent girl to work in a brothel.

'Readers may think I satirize intellectuals in my writing. If that is true, then I'm the first target of the satire,' Li Er has said. 'I'm familiar with life on campus. I'm familiar with intellectuals and how they behave. I write about them as if I were writing about myself. Intellectuals are the nerves of a culture. They are the sensors of a culture. Their feelings are complicated and I like to write about complexity. Writing about intellectuals fulfils my interest.'[7]

Writing about complexity is not an easy task for a writer in China, and being able to read pain means not only is Li Er refusing to self-anaesthetize, he also has to cope with feelings of powerlessness.

'I sense powerlessness all the time. It means that you know your resistance will not have any effect. It means failure strikes even before any action is taken,' Li told me. However, he also insists that 'to honestly write about how I feel makes me a real person. That's why I write. And I believe this is a moral principle for me as a writer.'[8]

'But what if there is a clash between what you want to say and what is allowed to be published?' I asked.

'Every writer in China who is serious about writing experiences this clash,' he replied. 'Chinese writers have been subjected to this clash since the days of Lu Xun. Of course, I will have to make adjustments, blurring references of the era, deleting some sensitive words, for example, but Chinese readers will understand what I really want to say.'

When I asked why both *The Magician of 1919* and *Coloratura* contain a magician, Li Er explained, 'I was fascinated by magicians when I was a little boy. Later I learned that magicians are in fact on the bottom rung of our society. Their job is just to entertain people. Even though it appears that nothing is impossible for magicians, they can never change their own status in the society.' That theme of powerlessness again.

Thinking about Li's comments on the pain and powerlessness experienced by Chinese intellectuals, including himself, I asked, 'Will you stay in China if you have a chance to leave?'

'I will definitely stay in China and write.'

For Li Er, staying close to his subjects and writing about them is non-negotiable, despite the pain and powerlessness.

Notes

[1] Li Er & Ma Ji 李洱，马季, 'Examining the plight of intellectuals throughout history and in the present day' (tan jiu zhi shi fen zi zai li shi he xiang shi zhong de kun jing 探究知识分子在历史和现实中的困境), *Writer* 作家杂志, 2007, (1).

[2] 'Mo Yao and Li Er win the first 21st Century Ding Jun Biennial Literary Prize' (Mo yan li er huo shou jie 21 shi jin ding jun shuang nian wen xue jiang 莫言、李洱获首届"21世纪鼎钧双年文学奖), *Writer Magazine* (zuo jia 作家), 2003 (3), pp. 6–8.

[3] Wang Hongtu 王宏图, 'About Li Er' (Li Er lun 李洱论)，(wen yi zheng ming 文艺争鸣), 2009 (4), p. 120.

[4] Li Er's interview with Wu Hongfei 吴虹飞 for *Southern People Weekly* (nan fang ren wu zhou kan 南方人物周刊), 23 March 2009, p. 77.

[5] Ibid., p. 78.

[6] Ibid.

[7] Wei Tianzhen 魏天真's interview with Li Er: 'Listen to the heartbeat of the world — Li Er interview' (qing ting shi jie de xin tiao Li Er fang tan lu 倾听到世界的心跳 — 李洱访谈录) *xiao shuo ping lun* 小说评论, 2006 (4), p. 27.

[8] Li Er's speech 'Why I write, what to write and how to write — speech at the Novelists' Forum hosted by

Suzhou University' (wei shen mo xie xie shen mo zen mo xie zai su zhou da xue xiao shuo jia jiang tan shang de jiang yan 为什么写, 写什么, 怎么写 — 在苏州大学"小说家讲坛"上的讲演), in *Contemporary Writers Review* (dang dai zuo jia ping lun 当代作家评论), 2005 (3), p. 47.

About the Translators

Jane Weizhen Pan is a native speaker of Mandarin and Cantonese and has an MA in translation studies from Monash University, and has taught translation and interpreting at RMIT University. Jane is currently a PhD candidate at the Australian National University researching nonsense literature. Jane and Martin Merz co-translated *English*, a novel by Wang Gang, published by Penguin in 2009. Her current project is translating a puppet show script adapted from *Alice's Adventures in Wonderland* into Mandarin and Cantonese.

Martin Merz hails from Melbourne, Australia, where he first began learning Chinese. He went to several language schools in Taiwan where he discovered that academia had not prepared him to bargain for bananas at the local market. In the early 1990s Martin translated a modern Peking Opera for fun. An MA in applied translation at the Open University of Hong Kong rekindled his interest in literary translation. He has co-translated, with Jane Weizhen Pan, *English* by Wang Gang, and a seventeenth-century opera by Li Yu, which was recently performed at the Fringe in Hong Kong.

Modern Chinese Masters

Yu Li: Confessions of an Elevator Operator

by Jimmy Qi

Biting satire...Beneath the humour, serious issues simmer. Time Out

Yu Li is an inspector at a fake wine distillery in a small town without any tall buildings in Hebei province. After he is fired for drinking the wine during his inspections, Yu Li manages to land another job as an elevator operator in a luxury apartment building in the far-off capital, Beijing.

The apartment building is home to the winners in the new China: celebrities, the new rich, and big-shot officials. Misadventures abound as Yu Li struggles to adjust to the confusion of city life and above all to subdue the 'nuclear weapon' in his pants.

ISBN: 978-988-18419-1-9

Make-Do Publishing

Modern Chinese Masters

I Love My Mum

by Chen Xiwo

One of contemporary China's most outspoken voices on freedom of expression for writers. Asia Sentinel

I Love My Mum is a shocking tale of murder and incest and a powerful metaphor for corruption in modern Chinese society. The story is narrated by a hardened vice squad detective who is used to the seamy side of life. But even he has never come across a murder case like this. And the same is guaranteed for the reader.

ISBN: 978-988-18419-2-6

Make-Do Publishing

Modern Chinese Masters

Forthcoming Title:

The Road of Others

by Anni Baobei

I felt that I had been walking through a long dark tunnel to the exit from a dream and it was time for a new beginning.

Anni Baobei is a cult Chinese writer whose fictions generally turns around characters detached from life in big industrialised cities. Her fiction is celebrated for its romantic, artistic and individualistic characteristics, which prompt love among her passionate fanbase.

Lin and Vivian develop an obsessive online relationship. For Vivian, the virtual pleasures of their friendship would be compromised if the 'game' became 'real' but Lin's determination to find Vivian becomes a destructive passion.

Make-Do Publishing